PRAISE FOR BOSS & HUNKY

Through the thought process of HUNKY, Andrea subtly and powerfully weaves in the need to speak up, have the self confidence to promote your ideas, and trust that you can reinvent yourself to deliver what you think.

—Francis "Brig" Bowe, MBA, Villanova '90
Retired Assistant Dean, Rosemont College

Andrea Mower writes with beauty, flair, and humor. Boss and Hunky is a book for young readers, but the lessons are for every age group and should be used as required reading for all human resource professionals. Handling change in our lives can present fear and issues, but as Andrea writes, "It is OK to let go." The illustrations by Robert Bahn are fabulously creative.

—Beverly Wichman, The Saucy Sisters
Author of *The Saucy Sisters Guide to Wine…What Every Girl Should Know Before She Uncorks* and *The Everything Wine Book*

The book enlightened me about the power of friendships and family. I am a firm believer that when you feel like a hot mess, the day gets better when you believe you are never alone.

—Dr. Barbara Collins
Midlife Transition Expert and
Author of *It's Your Turn* and *Power in Midlife and Beyond*

You know when you haven't seen someone in a while but when you do, you immediately reconnect, and it feels like no time has passed at all? That's the powerful feeling I get from this book! Embrace your place but trust the dust. That magical dust you leave behind with every person (or gargoyle) you encounter—the ones you call family, by blood or by choice, the ones you share a lifelong friendship or just a brief smile with, the magic found within all of us if only we dare to embrace ourselves, flaws and all, courageously! Andrea Mower brilliantly uses metaphors in such a relatable way throughout this book. I thoroughly enjoyed "Boss & Hunky: The Adventures of an Out-of-Work Gargoyle" and you will too! #trustthedust

—Blaze Kelly Coyle
CEO & Founder, Silver Phoenix Entertainment and
Author of *The Most Well Traveled Squirrel in the Whole Wide World*

BOSS & HUNKY

The Adventures of an
Out-of-Work Gargoyle©

ANDREA MOWER

Illustrated by Robert Bahn

For Tim

CONTENTS

FOREWORD

Change at any age, in any given situation, is never easy. Even when we know it is necessary, the fear of the unknown and the comfort of the known tend to keep us from stepping on the gas pedal of life. Add negative assumptions to the equation and the gas in our engines solidifies, jelling into a murky substance that glues us to our now and fogs our window of possibilities.

Whether out of work, out of the game, or outnumbered, we feel like an outcast. While it is unfortunate that such experiences do not end with childhood, it is even more unfortunate that some individuals do not mature with age. Andrea exploits this paradox perfectly, making the adventures in this book simultaneously trying, relatable, and delightful. She cleverly weaves personalities that we have either embodied or experienced at every stage of life, and her manner of revealing a 360-degree perspective keeps the pages turning.

Oh, to be Don with a bird's eye view of the world as it is!

Situations are not always as they appear. That concept, central to the storyline of *Boss & Hunky: The Adventures of an Out-of-Work Gargoyle*, challenges the casual observer's assumption that this is purely a book targeting youth. Intended or not, human nature is the actual subject. Who better to expose personalities, character strengths and flaws, and interpersonal relationships than an accomplished Human Resources professional?

The beauty of this adventure is that Andrea offers solutions, no doubt drawing upon her professional experiences and oodles of interpersonal relationships she has managed. Both our hero and heroine free themselves from their own limiting beliefs when they change their perspectives, and the magic happens when they trust their sage friend, each other, and ultimately themselves. Imagine applying such a simple concept to our personal lives, to our teams, to our organizations.

We have a choice: remain in a safe backyard with a motley crew in a never-ending cycle of bloom-and-wither or venture to the limitless horizon constantly facing new challenges where change always promotes growth.

Enjoy this fanciful read and be inspired.

Lorraine Ranalli

INTRODUCTION

Boss and Hunky Punk are gargoyles; you need to know this from the start. This story follows their journey. Boss yearns to find where she really belongs. Hunky Punk appears to have it all, but leads a lonely life. Will Boss ever find her purpose? Will Hunky Punk languish forever? How do you define family? What is home? Just because you are born a gargoyle, does that mean that you can only do gargoylie things?

CHAPTER ONE

Boss and Hunky Punk (Hunky for short) sit atop a very old building in the City of Metanoia. They've been there since the building was erected over 200 years earlier. Boss, a girl, and Hunky, a boy, are very happy. They never tire of their aerial view.

Many people come by to look up at them and take their pictures. They sit up there and look out at the vast sky and the people below. On rainy days, Boss is not in the mood for onlookers, but Hunky makes time for the people below.

Hunky always looks the same no matter the weather. Hunky has great big paws, a flowing mane, sharp teeth, large wings and a long tail. Despite being made out of cement, he appears to be furry. Boss, is similar in size to Hunky, but she has smaller wings and even sharper teeth. She is also made out of cement, but appears to have glistening scales, especially during a rainfall.

Pigeons sit with them from time to time, and they all talk and laugh with one another. Even when wire-netting was hung to deter the pigeons, Boss and Hunky found a way to remove it by tearing it down with icicles that were razor sharp. A lot of icicles form on Boss, but just a few are found on Hunky in the winter. The pigeons bring news and information to them from all over the world. This is how Boss and Hunky have been educated. This is also how they find out everything that is going on!

On a beautiful and brisk autumn day, their favorite pigeon of all, Don, brought them some terrible news.

"Guessss what? This old building is gonna be torn down to make way for brand newwww condos!" he exclaimed, pausing on the words guess and new for dramatic effect, like he often did.

"Condos?" they chimed in unison, and then Boss continued, "What is a condo?"

Don explained that right now a lot of people live in the old building, but when the condos are built, twice as many people can live there. Boss and Hunky had been sitting at the top of the building for over two centuries, and they didn't know what this news meant for their future.

As the days passed, Boss and Hunky watched a lot of activity below. A great big fence was wrapped around the entire old building. They watched as all of the people inside the old building came out with boxes and bags and cases in their arms. One after another, the people came out of the building. Mrs. Fleming had three cats in one carrier, and they were making such a racket, Boss couldn't help to think they were very upset they were leaving their home. Boss and Hunky watched and watched many people come out. Finally, Mr. Tidewater, the man in charge of the whole building, came out and closed the great big entry door and locked it. He wiped his eyes with a blue-and-white cloth he pulled out of his back pocket. He looked up to the top of the building and just shook his head. He walked down the street with his head hanging down and never looked back. Then the building was very quiet. Even the pigeons were gone. It was just Boss and Hunky. They missed the people and the animals. There were no more dogs on leashes coming out and going back in the building several times a day, let alone the people who lived there. It was too quiet and Hunky and Boss were very sad.

Early the next morning, they awoke to a lot of noise, even for the city! There was banging and clanking, and an annoying beeping sound every time one of the trucks below would back up. Suddenly, a giant yellow beak that was attached to the long neck of a bird approached Boss. Hunky watched as she was removed from the old building! She was now inside the beak of this strange bird! Where was Don when they needed him? Then, to Hunky's dismay, he watched her ear fall to the ground below! He looked down and it was shattered into many pieces. The next thing he knew, Boss was gone.

Then it was Hunky's turn. The bird beak, which was really just a big machine, approached him. "Be more careful with this one, they fetch a lot of money," yelled a man who wore a mask over his nose and mouth, to a masked man who was the driver of the bird machine.

The gargoyles were gone.

Discussion Questions

Describe a time when you were faced with major change at home, school, or in the workplace.

Was the change sudden or did you have time to digest it?

If you were able to prevent or stall the change, how did you accomplish this? What did you do?

If you were not able to prevent or stall the change, how did you learn to cope with it?

CHAPTER TWO

Boss and Hunky woke up to find themselves sitting in a large concrete yard, not too far from the old building. It was the first time they had been this close together in a long, long time. The last time they were right next to one another was when they were being created. The men who were wearing the masks and another man, who looked old and frail, were talking. The frail man circled both Boss and Hunky, inspecting them as though he was a judge in a fancy dog show. His face was emotionless until he stopped in front of Boss and raised the right corner of his upper lip in a gesture of disapproval. It was clear he did not fancy the gargoyle with a broken ear, and would only buy Hunky.

The frail man pointed to Hunky and said, "I'll take this one! Deliver it to my house tomorrow." Then he shuffled away without another word. The men looked at one another and shrugged their shoulders.

"Never know what these wealthy collectors are going to buy!" said one.

"What do we do with this one?" remarked the other, pointing to Boss with his thumb.

"Leave it," replied the first man as they walked away. "They will grind it up and use it as part of the foundation for the building, I suppose."

Boss and Hunky sat in silence for a long time before talking to one another. Hunky was wondering why the man, whose name must be Wealthy Collector, only wanted him, but not Boss. Boss did not comprehend her own fate at the moment; she only worried about being away from Hunky.

Boss broke the silence, "I am really going to miss you Hunky."

Hunky responded, "I am going to miss you too."

Boss looked at him closely, "You are bigger than I remember!"

"Speak for yourself!" Hunky answered, but he was actually thinking that she was prettier than he remembered.

After an awkward silence, they both began to speak at once. "Do you remember when-" They both laughed.

"Remember when those people got so wet!" reminisced Hunky.

Boss sighed, "Yeah, I will miss spitting water on the people below!"

"That is something I could never seem to do," Hunky thought to himself.

6

Boss sensed Hunky was feeling sad, so she quickly spoke up.

"That is why we came up with a game for both of us. Remember? But we needed so much patience…"

Hunky, feeling better, echoed "Sooo much patience."

Boss continued, "But in the early spring…"

Hunky completed her thought. "Those icicles…"

Boss added, "…hanging off our noses, would start to drip, drip, drip" and then, in unison, once again they chortled, "and then we would be back in business!"

Hunky added, "I loved watching the confused faces below!"

Boss, remembering, tilted her head up in the air and observed, "They'd look up and all around! Was it raining?"

They both laugh and then the awkward silence returned. Boss began to sob softly.

"Oh no, Boss, please don't do that. I don't know what to do with that," Hunky declared as he started to panic.

"I'm sorry, Hunky, but tomorrow you will be gone and I, I…will be rubble." Boss started bawling loudly. Dogs began barking in the distance, probably startled by her sobbing. Boss was finally comprehending her fate.

Hunky thought up something to say fast. "But, but, Boss, you will become many Bosses! There will be so much of you, that, that…"

Boss stopped crying for a moment and said, "That, what?"

Hunky panicked inside for a moment but then found the words to soothe her. "You will keep those new condos together. Before, you would divert rain water. So 17th century, but now…"

Boss echoed his last word, "Now?"

Confident in his story, Hunky replied, "Now you will be the foundation of homes for hundreds of people. And me?"

"And you?"

"I will be stared at by some crazy old rich guy who has nothing better to do with his money than buy a gargoyle!"

They both started giggling uncontrollably at the thought.

Boss reminded Hunky, "Well, you always wanted to be on stage!"

Silence fell between them again, but it was a comfortable silence. Boss finally broke the quiet, "Hunky...thanks."

Hunky replied awkwardly, "Boss?"

"Yeah, Hunky?"

"Nice ear!" They started giggling again uncontrollably until they both drifted off to sleep.

Discussion Questions

Have you ever encountered someone who felt undervalued by classmates, teammates, family, or coworkers?

List three things that you did or could do to make that person feel valued and appreciated.

Have you ever refused to purchase something because of a little flaw or defect, and then come to regret it later?

Have you ever consciously or subconsciously avoided a person (or refuse to hire someone) because of a perceived weakness without trying to get to know that person?

CHAPTER THREE

Light snow was falling, providing a backdrop for a flash of extraordinary lights. Deep purples and magentas turned a black sky to royal blue. The wind started to howl, and the snow turned to glitter or even diamonds. Boss' eyes opened wide. Suddenly she lifted her right front leg and was astonished. Then she lifted her left front leg. Her great big tail started to sway. She rose off the ground slightly, her back legs dangling in the air, just a foot or so off the ground. She floated back down gently, and the four pads of her paws crunched into the freshly fallen, glittering snow. Then, as if she had done this her entire life, she started to slowly walk toward the gate at the fence. A dog bounded toward her, with bared teeth and drool flying, but then the dog stopped dead in his tracks and let Boss tap the gate lightly with her front paw. She simply walked out of the gate. Hunky, still frozen in place, never awakened.

Boss' search for something other than being rubble had begun.

She started to wander down the street tentatively at first but gradually picked up speed. She looked back at the building she called home for so long and knew she could never go back there again. She looked over to where Hunky remained sitting, covered in snow, but quickly turned away and pushed him out of her mind for fear she would feel too sad. She didn't know where she was going, but she knew she had to find a new home…and a new purpose! This is something, she figured, people call a job. What was she going to do all day?

As Boss made her way down the street, she noticed that seemingly inanimate objects came to life, just as she passed by. Door knockers—lions, rams, and eagles—would smile, wink, or even snarl at her. She was excited and frightened all at the same time. Lawn ornaments waved hello or curtsied. One pleasant-looking ornament tipped his top hat to her. A boar's head on a tavern sign gave her a big grunt followed by a wink. She didn't know whether to be scared or flattered.

Boss journeyed on late into the night and to the beginning of a new day. She realized the faster she walked, the more she could rise off the ground and fly. The tiny wings on her back weren't just ornamental after all! She rose into the air and started to fly, but then she would abruptly land, and then try again. Her best pigeon friend, Don, spotted her and laughed.

"Boss, girrrrl, you need some flying lessons!"

She was so happy to see Don, she didn't even complain that

he stretched out his words for dramatic effect. Don gave out a big coo and suddenly there were dozens of pigeons everywhere and of every color - light grey, dark grey, brown, tan, white and blue, all helping Boss maintain herself in flight.

Don was yelling, "C'mon girl, flap those ridiculously small wings."

That just made Boss laugh and she landed on the ground again.

Don exclaimed, "Boss, that is enough for one day, you are hoofing it for now."

Don lifted his right wing to his beak and gave out another big coo and the entire flock was suddenly gone. Boss felt tired and a little discouraged, but she journeyed on. Don maintained a safe distance so Boss would not discover he was watching over her.

Discussion Questions

What hidden talent have you discovered about yourself?

Do you have a coach or a mentor who helps you from time to time?

CHAPTER FOUR

The quiet cement under her paws turned to the sound of crunching, and Boss found herself departing the cement road. She walked on a cobblestone street that quickly turned to gravel, and then to grass. Or was it a field? She stopped. Boss lifted her weary head and, to her astonishment, she saw a Help Wanted sign in front of an old, run down house. She was also astonished that she could read!

"Help Wanted – Haunted House" she read aloud.

The next month for Boss was glorious. She loved the colors

of autumn and the many visitors that came to the old house. She was situated on the front porch of an old Victorian manor. Children always patted the top of her head when they took that last step to the porch. Smaller children sometimes needed to grab her good ear for support so they could make that last steep step up to the porch. One little girl kissed her bad ear and put a kitten bandage on it. Boss loved the children. She loved her new home and she loved her new job. Teenagers used their phones to take selfies with her. Adults tweeted where they were. Boss didn't know what a tweet was, but she was sure Don could explain it to her the next time he flew by, being a bird and all.

The only thing missing was Hunky. She wished he was on the other side of the porch. Boss soothed herself, knowing he was living a rich and luxurious life. She reasoned that by this time, Hunky had probably forgotten about her anyway.

Discussion Questions

Describe the last time you felt as if you really fit in.

*On occasions when you might have felt like an outcast,
what specifically were you doing? Describe the people
you would have been among. Was it the task, people,
or both that made you feel as though it was not a good fit?*

CHAPTER FIVE

Hunky woke up from a long nap and looked around a very large, dark-paneled room. Soon the light flicked on, and his wealthy collector, WC, which Hunky called him for short, entered the room and began staring at him. Hunky had nothing to do all day but think and think, and then think some more. He thought about Boss almost all of the time.

"At least she is now the foundation for many people to live in many beautiful homes," he thought to himself. That thought would make him feel a little better. Other times, though, he would question the notion.

"So what if her ear was damaged?" The fact that WC rejected her simply made no sense to Hunky. Every time he thought about the look on her face when she realized she would not be going with him, he closed his eyes and squeezed them tightly in an attempt to erase the memory.

"It was a nick, a scratch really. A little imperfection."

"We were created centuries ago!"

"Give us a break."

"Hasn't anyone ever heard of glue before?"

Hunky knew he was crying, but it had been so long since he was near any moisture, no tears could actually flow. He missed water, and icicles and snow. Hunky's thoughts were interrupted by the glow of the light. WC, so skinny and frail, came shuffling into the room. WC stared at Hunky expressionlessly and Hunky stared back with even less expression.

Discussion Questions

Have you ever felt bored despite having a task to accomplish?

Describe ways in which you combat boredom.

Think about a time when you came to the defense of another person. How did you speak up for that person and to whom? What did you do to lift that person's spirits and help him or her regain confidence?

CHAPTER SIX

"Well, season's over," a lanky man in overalls declared.

Boss, confused, wondered what was happening. Don, who was perched on her head, clarified when the lanky man was out of earshot. "It's November 1st, Girl."

"What is a November 1st?" Boss replied.

"Halloween is overrrrr." And with that, Don flew away as he watched an unpleasant woman with a broom run towards him.

"Git!" she shrieked. Don left the unpleasant woman a special present on the step as he flew away.

"Clean that up lady!"

Boss couldn't believe it. This was her new home and her new job. Where were the children? Where were her noisy teenagers? A big van pulled up, and the haunted house workers quickly shoved everything that was in the house and on the porch into it.

"We will need a couple of big boys to lift this thing," a short man announced as he pointed to Boss.

"Thing? I'm a thing," she thought.

Before Boss could build up enough of her own momentum to just leave the porch, the lanky fella said, "Ah, it's too heavy to lift. Leave it. We will get it later."

Boss watched as the big van rolled away. One by one, she watched the other workers get in their cars and disappear. Then, it was quiet.

Boss spoke aloud, "Now what? Do I stay here or journey forward? Maybe someone will return."

Boss stayed on the porch for a month. She watched leaves fall off the trees and felt the weather turn colder and colder. She slept a lot. She thought a lot. She had the freedom to walk, run, or fly away, yet she remained. She thought out loud, "At least Hunky has someone. No one has looked at me for a month!" Her pigeon friend wasn't even coming by to check on her.

Boss was startled out of her sleep by a loud bang. A huge truck! What was that delightful smell? Trees! So many trees! A large man with a cigar hanging off his lower lip was shouting orders to two identical twin teenage boys. All the while, the cigar never fell out of his mouth. The two boys looked just like him, only younger.

"C'mon boys, we don't have all day!"

The boys looked at each other and rolled their eyes. The large man continued.

"I want those trees set up and this place to look like Merry Christmas by noon!"

The boys jumped into action and started to unload the trees from the huge truck.

This was very familiar to Boss. Once a year, her view below would be crowded with pine trees in the beginning of the month which would dwindle a little every day. By the end of the month, the trees were gone. Christmas. Yes, Christmas trees! Boss shut her eyes tight to help her remember the sounds of the bells coming from the church across the street.

Hunky would sing along with the bells but not know any of the words of the hymns. He would sing to the hymn of Silent Night, "I am right. I am right. Day or night, I am right!" Boss sighed and opened her eyes.

"Dad?" questioned one of the twins pointing directly at Boss. "What is…that?" Then he moved his finger closer to point right in her face.

"How in the world should I know?" the large man replied. "Move it to the back of the house!"

The boys tried to move Boss but she was too heavy and she wasn't helping them either. One twin exclaimed, "This thing won't budge!"

Boss thought to herself, "Again with the word, thing. I am not a thing!"

Flustered, the large man replied, "Then I don't know, stick a hat on it" and he stomped away.

The other twin, or perhaps the same one because she didn't know who was who, ran to the truck and returned with a red hat trimmed in white fur. He plopped it on her head.

"There!" he said with a smile. "We have our very own Christmas Elf!" His smile revealed a chipped front tooth.

"OK" Boss thought. "I will name him Twin One."

The other twin sneered, "Some elf," They both started to laugh.

The other twin did not have a chipped tooth. "I will name him Twin Two," thought Boss.

Boss remained on the porch as the "Elf," but it didn't really feel like the job fit. It did not have the same feeling to her as her Halloween job. Occasionally someone would take a picture with her, but she felt it was to make fun of her, instead of when pictures were taken of her at Halloween. Boss enjoyed watching the families pick out their trees. For about a week it was very busy, and she never got bored. She imagined what the homes of the families looked like, and wondered how they were going to decorate their trees.

Discussion Questions

*Why do you think Boss remained on the
porch after Halloween was over?*

*Have you ever remained somewhere or in a situation too long?
If so, what finally prompted you to make a change?*

What advice would you give others who might be reluctant to change?

CHAPTER SEVEN

Hunky was startled to find the dark paneled room was suddenly different. All the curtains and drapes were pulled back, and beams of light, and a lot of dust, filled the room. Many people came in to the room and were bustling about: cleaning, wiping, and polishing the enormous space back to what, Hunky could only imagine, was its original glory. One of the ladies was coughing and opened a window so the dust could escape. The room felt happy for the first time since Hunky arrived.

By nightfall, dozens of people poured into the room. Hunky

enjoyed all the sights and sounds: the clinking of glasses, the talking, and the laughter. As these people moved around the room, he wondered to himself, "Where is WC? Who are all of these people?"

"How does he know so many people?"

A young couple approached Hunky and broke his train of thought. "Oh, a gargoyle!" the young woman exclaimed.

"It's actually a Hunky Punk," replied the young man with a thick accent he never heard before.

"A hunk what?" she replied.

The young man went on, "It is built to look just like the gargoyle but it serves only an ornamental purpose."

"Oh, well I like it!" She asserted while smiling at Hunky. "He's so, so…" She stopped to find the correct word.

"Grotesque?" replied the young man.

"Yes, that, but beautiful all at the same time! I wonder where he came from?" Her voice was trailing off as they walked away from Hunky, but she kept looking back over her shoulder at him.

Dismayed, Hunky thought to himself. "Well, that explains it. I serve no purpose other than to be looked at. Now it makes perfect sense that I am here. This is where I am meant to be."

Suddenly the activity didn't seem fun to him anymore. He thought about Boss and how every time it rained she was busy with the water spouting out of her mouth and couldn't talk to him, but he never had any water to dispose.

"She's the gargoyle, and I am the…" Now he was at a loss for words.

"Look-alike? Did she invent the icicle game to spare my feelings?"

Hunky started to get his resolve back and thought to himself, "Well, I may be purely ornamental, but I'm a good citizen, well, when I wasn't dripping my icicles on people below…with Boss."

Before Hunky knew it, the room was empty again. And dark. The drapes were drawn and every sign of life was gone.

Discussion Questions

Hunky felt like he had no purpose in life.
What advice would you give someone who felt that way?

Why do you think Boss invented the icicle game?

Would you invent or make up something just to
make someone feel better? Why or why not?

CHAPTER EIGHT

Boss decided not to stay at the Victorian manor beyond Christmas. She was not about to watch one more truck roll away from her. As much a she enjoyed watching the families buy the trees, she knew once the tree supply dwindled, she would, once again, be alone. Boss waited until it was dark and Twin Two was on watch. He was the lazy one who always slept through the entire night instead of guarding the trees. She would wind up guarding the trees for him and stay up all night. She felt the need to guard and to protect.

Boss went to lift her front right paw and could not move it. She tried the front left. Her left paw would not move either. She realized she couldn't move anything. She started to panic. It had been so long since she tried to move, that now she was unable.

"I could have left after Halloween but I stayed. Why did I stay?" Boss was stuck on the front porch of the dilapidated Victorian manor, perhaps forever. She decided to close her eyes and go to sleep. She didn't even feel like guarding the trees anymore.

"After all, who is going to come all the way out here to steal a tree?" And with that last thought, she closed her eyes and fell into a deep sleep.

A month went by, and the truck was back. She felt a breeze over her head as her red and white hat was lifted off. Twin One carried the hat to the truck. The large man, Twin One, and Twin Two loaded the last remaining trees in the truck. Then they were gone. She was alone again. It was very quiet, and the air was still. Boss felt helpless and stuck. She longed to fly again. If only she could, she would finally leave and find a new home and new work.

Discussion Questions

Can you recall a time when you had to do someone else's work because they were lazy or incompetent? Were your efforts appreciated or acknowledged?

If you could have a do-over, would you handle that situation differently? If so, how?

CHAPTER NINE

Hunky was confused about all the people who were in the room that one evening. He also wanted to know where WC was and he was dismayed that WC didn't show him off to his guests. The window that was used to let the dust escape remained open, and the curtain started to flutter. Suddenly, the wind howled, and snow swirled into the room. Hunky looked out the window and was amazed to see the most beautiful purple and royal blue sky. Confused by everything, Hunky scratched his head. Then he realized, he could scratch his head! He tentatively tilted his head slightly to the left and then, with more confidence, to the right.

"I can...move?" He lifted his left paw but then heard the door open. "Oh darn," he said and realized his voice was too loud.

WC shuffled in and muttered to himself, "Who left that window open?"

Try as he might, WC could not close the window. He called for someone named Morton, and a stiff-looking man came in. WC motioned to the window without a word and the stiff man shut the window and latched it, and drew the curtains shut with what Hunky thought was a little too much of a dramatic flourish. The stiff man then nodded to WC, expressionless, and left the room. Hunky realized the dramatics were because the stiff man was in his pajamas and probably asleep when he was summoned.

WC sighed. Hunky asked, "Are you OK?" and then realized what he had done.

WC's eyes grew wide. He looked all around the room with only his eyes and then shook his head as if he had imagined another voice. WC started to leave the room but then turned back to look at Hunky. It seemed as if he looked at Hunky for a very long time. Hunky was worried that this could be his only opportunity to move. As soon as the snow landed on Hunky, he changed. Something happened to him. Hunky squeezed his eyes shut and then opened them very wide.

Hunky swallowed and then verbalized, out loud, "Sir, it was me who spoke." WC whirled around to find the voice and stopped when he looked at Hunky's face.

"Am I going crazy?" WC exclaimed.

"No." Hunky replied. "Please don't be scared. I don't know what is going on either."

WC let out a little gasp and then collapsed onto the floor. "Oh great," Hunky lamented, "what did I do?"

Hunky wiggled off of his platform and jumped down to the floor. He took his front right paw and gently patted WC's face. Hunky sat vigil over him until WC finally sat up and they were face to face.

"I won't hurt you. You are my family now," Hunky whispered.

WC was still very confused, but no longer felt like he was in danger. After a moment, Hunky continued, in a louder voice. "Hi, I am Hunky Punk, Hunky for short."

WC didn't say anything; he just stared at Hunky in amazement. Hunky felt awkward, but he went on, "You bought a gargoyle, well I'm not technically a gargoyle. The gargoyle, her name is Boss, yes, she is a girl…is gone. She had a broken ear."

WC nodded and then stood up and was straightening his pants and then his shirt. After fiddling with his outfit for a while, he finally said, "Hi Hunky, I'm Walter Christensen."

Hunky thought to himself, "He really is WC!"

"I only had room here for one of you." Hunky looked at him skeptically, and then around the vast room that could fit dozens of gargoyles. Walter sensed Hunky's reaction, "And I guess I am particular, so I bought you instead of a broken one."

Walter suddenly felt terribly insensitive and asked, "Did I break up a family?"

"No, well, yes." Hunky replied. He went on to explain to Walter how long they had known one another. "Boss and some pigeons, I guess, are the only family I have ever known, uh I mean, that is until you." Hunky's shoulders suddenly slumped.

Walter responded, "I see." He paused between thoughts but then continued, "I have no family at all." Hunky asked about the people at the party. Walter replied, "Oh, that." Walter explained that he rents out his home from time to time to the city for important events like fundraisers and charity auctions.

"They want my house, Hunky, not me," Walter stated matter-of-factly. Hunky suddenly realized that he and Walter were very similar. They both felt like they had no one. They wound up talking for such a long time that Hunky noticed the light changing periodically in the room.

They sat on the floor together and leaned against Hunky's platform. Walter shared his life story.

"My full name is Walter Charles Christensen. My parents came here from a country halfway around the world. My father had nothing, he was penniless, but he made his fortune in the oil industry. My mother was a school teacher, but after I was born and then my sister, she stayed home. My little sister died when she was very young. My mother wasn't quite the same after that but…she was a wonderful mother. She was just a little delicate. My parents sent me to all of the best schools because my father, despite his wealth, never had much of a formal education."

Hunky didn't quite understand what a formal education was, but he understood most of Walter's story. "I met my wife, Anna Marie, when we were very young. In fact, she used to live right next door to this house. We met in Sunday school after the teacher threw me out into the hallway for making too much noise during class. She walked by to return to her classroom, and we bumped into each other. I loved her from the day I almost knocked her over."

Walter stopped talking for a while. Hunky didn't say a word either. Walter continued. "My mother loved her too, and Anna Marie became like a daughter to her. Anna Marie took care of my mother when she was dying." Again, there was silence for a long time.

Walter finally continued and revealed, "Anna Marie and I were together for 60 years. When Anna Marie died, a part of me died as well. One of the reasons I bought you…. Oh Hunky, I'm sorry, this sounds so inappropriate now."

Walter started over. "One of the reasons I wanted you in my home is because the first movie we saw together was about a hunchback. A love story really. There were gargoyles in the movie. We loved going to the movie house, and it only cost a dollar to see cartoons and two full-length features."

Hunky didn't understand what a dollar was or a lot of what Walter was talking about, but his story interested him all the same, and he could tell that Walter was a very loving man.

"So, Hunky, I'm all alone now and I have been for a long time. I have staff."

Walter looked at Hunky and realized his expression had turned to confusion.

"I have people who I pay to take care of the house and cook."

Hunky nodded because he understood Walter must have bought them, too. He wondered if everyone, including him, cost a dollar or if a dollar was only used to see a movie. As Hunky wondered, Walter observed, more to himself than to Hunky, "I guess I bought them, too."

Walter went on to explain further to Hunky, "I pay them, but they work for it. They are good workers and nice people. They don't have to talk to me, but they do."

Walter sighed and stopped talking. He had not talked that much in quite a while and was feeling very tired.

Walter and Hunky sat together for a long time. Both were dozing on and off. Walter finally stood up and looked at Hunky. "Now what?"

Hunky stood up as well. Walter continued, "Obviously, you are free to go."

Hunky didn't move.

"Heck, you could trample me if you like," Walter worried while examining how muscular Hunky was.

"No, Walter, sir." Walter just seemed like a Sir to Hunky. "I don't want to do that, but I do need to go and pay my respects to Boss." Walter understood.

"The concrete, which was made into rubble, contains my friend, and I want to say goodbye to her."

Walter opened the door to the room and led Hunky to the enormous front doors. He opened them wide.

"Hunky, you are welcome to return here any time you like."

Hunky smiled a crooked grin at Walter, and Walter realized he was grotesque and beautiful all at the same time.

"Thank you, Walter," Hunky said as he walked out the door.

"I'm sorry, Hunky," Walter murmured with his head down. Walter added, "I bet Boss was wonderful."

Walter shut the enormous doors. As Hunky walked down the front steps, he thought to himself, "She was. She really was."

Discussion Questions

Have you ever had a "snow moment" (an Ah-ha moment), where it seemed everything in your life changed? What was that like?

How would you guide others to find their "snow moment"?

Would you encourage someone to make a change or resign their position even though it might inconvenience you?

CHAPTER TEN

"Hrrrugh!" Suddenly Boss was lifted by three very large men, and they shuffled their feet very quickly to move her to the back of the Victorian manor. They set her down gently in the middle of what appeared to have been a garden at one time. Boss looked around at the overgrown weeds, broken flower pots, and statuary and imagined to herself what the garden must have looked like a long time ago. Boss knew something about gardens. She always had a bird's eye view of two beautiful gardens: one just below her building and the other across the street at the church.

"This is not a garden," she thought to herself. "These are weeds." She remembered the perfectly manicured grass. Everything was so green and lush near her old home. Even in the winter, the holly bushes, ivy, and evergreen trees didn't lose their beauty.

Once the large men were out of earshot, she declared, "That's it. I am leaving tonight, snow or no snow." It wasn't quite spring yet, but it was unusually warm for this time of year.

After the sun went down and Boss made sure no one was around, in preparation for her next journey, she lifted her front right paw and stretched out her toes until she could actually see her large pointy toe nails. She did exactly the same with her front left paw, followed by her two back feet.

"Well, that is enough for one day." She said aloud. She spent the next several days dozing in the garden and did not try to stretch her paws again.

It didn't take too long for Boss to realize the Victorian manor was going to become somebody's real home. Not a Halloween attraction. Not a Christmas tree lot. A real home with a real family living inside of it. So Boss was determined to stay just a little bit longer because she was so curious to see the new people. She wondered if the manor would actually turn into her forever home. After all, she was not thrown away, she was moved to the garden, or what could become a garden again. She was placed in the center of the garden. Perhaps being placed in the center meant something special.

Boss watched as a flurry of new activity took over the house during the next several days. A big truck parked outside one morning, and about five different people made dozens of trips from the house to the truck. They removed a lot of items that were inside the home and loaded them into the truck. Then another big truck arrived, and people unloaded items, bringing the stuff into the home! Boss couldn't understand why items went out—couches, chairs, beds—but then items went back in that looked so similar to the couches, chairs, and beds that had gone out.

On a day that was very dreary and dismal, Don flew in and sat right on top of Boss' head.

"Girrrl you have been here for-ev-er!" he exclaimed, emphasizing the word forever for dramatic effect. "What is going on with you?" he demanded.

Boss looked up at him and almost went cross-eyed because he was right on the center of her head.

"I've been waiting to see…what happens," she responded timidly.

"You've been stuck, that's what you've been," he retorted.

Boss rolled her eyes.

"Don't you roll your eyes at me, girl! I'm looking down at you, and I can see exactly what you are doing!"

"Don, I could have left, but I guess I sort of gave up." Boss was surprised that saying it out loud made her feel better. "I think that maybe this can be my forever home," she added before he could get another word in.

"Girl, I will be back the very next time it snows. You know what I mean." And with that, he flew away.

Boss did know what he meant. Don helped her the first time, and she was afraid that if he came back and she was unwilling to go, it would be her last chance.

Discussion Questions

Have you ever stayed in an uncomfortable position hoping it might improve, even though you knew deep down that it would not?

Do you think Don was an "I told you so" friend or a friend who tried to give Boss the distance she needed to make her own decisions?

CHAPTER ELEVEN

The weeks went by at the Victorian manor and Boss was delighted to see the house come to life. The family painted the house many colors—burgundy, mauve, pink, and white. It looked to her like the big, beautiful cakes she would see down on the street-level at her old building from time to time, carried by men in tall, white hats. Boss could hear laughter from the house. There was a tall slender man, a tiny lady, and three very small children. She thought there were two boys and a girl, but she was not sure. Many people came and went, and there was a lot of noise during the day: banging, sawing, and drilling. They were noises she was used to hearing in the city. She loved all the activity.

The garden came to life as well. The weeds were pulled and flowers started to bloom. Other statuary was added to the garden. There was a little man with a pipe and a pointed hat, a turtle, an angel, and a fairy. One frosty evening, they all discovered everyone could come to life at night! They were all able to talk to one another. No one left the property, but everyone could move around freely within the garden. The angel and fairy could also fly, but they never seemed to fly more than about four feet off the ground. Most of the time, they walked instead.

At first, Boss enjoyed her new companions, but then bickering began. There were little arguments at first about what flower was blooming or some other unimportant fact. One night, the little man with the pointed hat and pipe, who she discovered was called a gnome, leaned over to look at her more closely and asked, "Hey, what happened to your ear?"

Boss had almost forgotten about her ear by now but answered, "It broke when they took me off my building." Boss suddenly felt self-conscious in front of the others.

The gnome continued, "You are about the ugliest thing I've ever seen, and that broken ear does not help." He laughed, thinking others would laugh as well. Boss was more hurt by the word thing than the word ugly. She wondered why he would even say that. Was he angry because she was placed in the center of the garden?

The angel came to Boss' defense and sweetly made clear to the gnome, "Now, that is not a nice way to talk."

The turtle tucked his head in his shell because that is all he ever did, even when they argued.

The fairy snorted, "Shorty with the hat is right. She is ugly!"

The angel was shocked that the fairy would say that, and

asked to have a word with her privately. After a few minutes, the fairy returned and apologized to Boss. But it was too late. Boss longed for her true friend, Hunky, and her feathered friend, Don, and snow. How long until the snow would return? She fantasized that Hunky would come barreling into the garden and give everyone a big roar, snarling at them with all of his sharp teeth. That would show them! She knew thinking about it was of no use. It was never going to happen.

Discussion Questions

Do you recognize anyone in the garden from your own friend or work group? Identify among your circle of influence the

Angel:

Fairy:

Gnome:

Turtle:

How have you dealt with a person who has insulted you? Did your method work? Why or why not?

CHAPTER TWELVE

Hunky wandered the streets. He had no idea where to go. He had no sense of direction. Hunky felt like he was walking for days. He didn't even know he could fly until Don flew by, circled around, and came face to face with Hunky.

"Well, well, well. Decided to leave the good life?"

Hunky's heart leapt for joy when he saw his old friend.

"Don, I've missed you!" exclaimed Hunky.

Don shook his head, which always looked like it was turning all the way around, and trilled, "Boyyy, I have so much to tell you!"

Don explained to Hunky exactly where Boss was, how long she had been there, everything she went through, and her current dilemma in the garden.

Hunky interrupted Don and asked, "How do you know so much?"

Don laughed at Hunky. "I've had a nest in the tree about five feet from Boss all along!" Don went on. "Do you think I would just leave her all alone?"

Hunky was surprised and said, "What about your own family?"

"You and Boss are my family. Besides, trees have branches, Hunky. My whole gang came with me after that old building was torn down!"

Hunky smiled.

"We have our own neighborhood in that tree!" reasoned Don, laughing. "Now, let's go to that garden, Hunky. She needs you."

It seemed like an eternity of walking to Hunky. He also realized that he had grown accustomed to the quiet at Walter's house. Don's non-stop talking and fluttering around his head was making Hunky quite nervous. Hunky suppressed his feelings because he knew Don was there to help. Light turned to darkness. Darkness turned to light. It was nearly nightfall again when a house, way in the distance, finally came into view. It was just as Don described. Hunky wondered why someone painted a house pink. His thoughts were interrupted by shouting behind the house. Hunky ran past the house and stopped short when the garden was practically in front of him. Don motioned for him to duck behind his tree to watch what was going on.

Hunky observed what he thought was the most unusual set up in a garden. It was nothing like the gardens he could see from his building long ago. The gardens he was used to had beautifully manicured trees and shrubs, long gravel paths, and flowers planted in neat little rows. He saw Boss in the center, various flowers and bushes, and a variety of statuary. He spotted an angel, which was very familiar to him because the church across the street from his old building had angels near the top of the building. Hunky smiled because the angel seemed so sweet. Then he saw a green-eyed fairy who looked ornery. Then he saw the back of the little man with the pointed hat. He didn't understand why his hat looked like a big red cone. He then saw the turtle.

Everyone was bickering. The angel was trying to keep the peace, the little man was shouting, the turtle kept putting his head inside his shell, and the fairy seemed to take sides with the angel and then with the little man and then with the angel again. In the center of it all was Boss and she looked miserable.

Hunky was just about to bound forward like the half lion he was, but Don stopped him. "Nooo, Hunky. Let's be smart. These others will be here forever. I've been watching them for a long time…they come to life at night, but it doesn't seem like they can leave the garden."

Hunky didn't care, he just wanted to get Boss out of there.

Don continued, "Hunky, we need to wait for the first snow fall. Then we can get her out. If they all discover the snow as well, we might be stuck with them all forever. We need to get her out quietly."

Hunky understood, although he didn't like it.

Discussion Questions

Think of a time you wanted to spring into action but were advised otherwise. Was it better to wait and strategize? What was the result?

Think of a time you did spring into action. What was the result? Would you do it again?

Who do you think the garden characters represent among your circle of influence?

CHAPTER THIRTEEN

Hunky watched Boss every night. During the day, he would duck behind Don's tree or hide in the nearby field. Whatever it was that grew in the field was thick and tall, and he was able to hide well, even when the man on the tractor came out to tend his fields. Don let Hunky know the man was a farmer from another home. He did not own the Victorian manor. Hunky would make sure he moved to a different spot every day so he would not leave a dent where he rested.

Spring changed to a blistering summer, which seemed to never end. Finally, the heat was gone and the leaves began to change to auburn, golden, and brown colors and cascade to the ground. It wouldn't be long now until winter. Don made sure Hunky remained patient. In the spring, Don distracted Hunky with all of the newly hatched birds from the tree. Don had six of his own that would sit on Hunky on a regular basis. Now Hunky had so much company, talking and fluttering, he was never bored. He grew to enjoy his extended and loud family.

Boss grew more and more lonely. Every night was the same. The little man would make fun of her in some way, or he would make fun of someone else. By the end of the night, the angel would teach everyone to be nice, but then it would happen all over again the next night. Boss realized that words don't always work if someone isn't willing to change their ways. Boss was bored, and it didn't even bother her anymore to be called a thing or to be called ugly. She even stopped looking up to the back of the house to watch the children play in the yard. She no longer cared. She didn't care about anything. She noticed some green fuzz on her sides and paws. The turtle explained it was moss. Sometimes she wished it would just grow over her completely, and she could become a part of the plant life. She wanted to disappear. She even stopped thinking about Hunky. Don was so busy keeping him entertained, as well as his six babies fed, that he forgot to check up on Boss.

One day, Hunky noticed the green fuzz on Boss' legs and asked Don about it. Don suddenly realized he had forgotten to check up on her.

"Hunky, watch my babies!" Don shrieked and with that, Don flew straight to the center of the garden and sat on top of Boss' head.

"Don?" Boss whispered.

"Oh, come on, girl, you know its me." But then Don realized, she didn't know. It had been too long. He had neglected his dear friend. He tried again.

"Yes Boss, I am here…and Hunky is too."

Her eyes darted around. "Where?"

"Well, he's hiding. We have a plan," Don replied.

"Hiding?" Boss exclaimed. "For how long? How long have you been here?"

Don realized that no matter what information he shared, his answer was not going to sound good to Boss. "Uhh" was all he could utter.

Boss said almost to herself, "No matter. I think this is where I belong now."

Don could not find the words to explain the plan. All he could think of was how horrible it was going to seem to her that they have been just a few feet away for months and months. Don flew back to Hunky without saying another word to Boss.

Discussion Questions

Name your "green moss" (stuck) moment.

What did you do to shake loose?

Even while raising his enormous family, Don seems to get things done. How do you treat people who have priorities outside your team/class?

How have you been treated when your personal priorities take precedence over the team's/class's?

CHAPTER FOURTEEN

Nightfall. Again. Bickering, followed by apologies. Sleep. When everyone was finally silent, Don told Hunky about Boss.

"Hunky, what can I say to her?"

Hunky thought for a moment. "She knows I'm here right?"

"Right," Don answered.

"Don, you told her we have a plan?"

"Yes." Don confirmed and nodded.

Hunky stood up and gave the biggest roar he could muster. It shook the tree and all of the dozing pigeons started flapping about. Don flew backward and landed on the ground on his tail feathers.

"What did you do that for?" Don exclaimed.

"She needs to know I am really here," Hunky simply commented and shut his eyes for the remainder of the night.

Boss knew. She knew everything at the moment she heard Hunky roar. She also knew she needed Don to come back so she could warn Hunky not to do it again. The last time they heard strange noises, the local farmers came out with long brown sticks and looked for the noise. The man in the Victorian manor joined them.

She kept saying under her breath, "Don, come back. Come see me."

Don kept watch over Hunky.

"If it isn't one, it's the other that I have to watch over," he muttered, but secretly, he was happy to be a part of their world, no matter how scary it had become. Don eventually dozed off along with his pigeon family. Their soft cooing kept Hunky asleep as well.

Boss, on the other hand, was wide awake and had a new determination about her. She knew she could not put her friends in harm's way if they attempted to rescue her. She thought a lot about how she became so complacent over the past several months, or was it years? At this point, she wasn't even sure how much time had passed since they were first removed from the building. She did know that she almost gave up.

"Well no more," Boss spoke with a newly found confidence. "I need to figure this out for myself, and then I can meet up with my friends and we can start a new life together!"

Discussion Questions

Was teamwork involved in rescuing Boss or did she do it on her own?

Describe your "well no more" moment at work or on a team.
Did you go it alone or was it a group effort?

.

CHAPTER FIFTEEN

Walter's head was resting on his pillow, but it was turned sideways to look out the window. Walter took to his bed right after Hunky left. He wasn't sure if he was actually ill or just feeling melancholy. Hunky brought excitement into his life. For a brief moment, Walter did not feel so alone. Walter hoped Hunky found his way back to the condos to pay his respects to his friend. He also hoped Hunky was doing well. The weather was getting colder and colder and Walter could feel rain or snow in his bones.

Boss looked up at the night sky and thought to herself that it was getting colder. She spoke aloud, "All I need is a good snow and I can finally leave."

Several days and nights went by without snow, but Boss kept her spirits up. Finally, the snow started to fall, gently at first, and then it started to snow harder. Boss tried with all of her might, but she just could not move.

Hunky was elated at the snowfall! He imagined Boss bounding at them at any moment! They would leave this place forever. He waited and waited, but Boss never showed. Despite the farmers with the long brown sticks, Hunky snuck back to the garden.

"No one is coming out in this weather," he thought. No one did. All of the statuary were frozen. The angel was looking up to the heavens, the fairy had that ornery look on her face, the little man's pointed hat was down across his eyes, and the turtle's head was inside his shell. Boss, in the center of it all, appeared to be frozen as well.

The wind started to howl. Hunky yelled out to Boss. "Come on, it is time to go!"

Boss wasn't sure at first if she heard him or it was just a dream. Hunky repeated himself. "It…is…time…to GO!"

Boss' head snapped around, and just like that she ran out of the garden, sliding slightly on the fresh snow.

"It's about time girl!" Don exclaimed from the tree and took off to catch up with Hunky.

She just needed a little reassurance that it really was time to go. It was OK to go. It was OK to let go. For just a brief moment she considered whether the snow had anything to do with it at all or was it something inside her all along. When she caught up to Hunky, he started to run.

"Let's go before the snow stops. We need to go somewhere first before we move on."

Don flapped his wings furiously to keep up in the storm.

Pride prevented Don from running, so with all of his might he kept pace with the gargoyles.

Boss was confused but did not care. She ran as fast as she could from the garden. She never looked back.

Discussion Questions

Was it the magical snow that allowed Boss and Hunky to move or was it their own determination?

Imagine your "never look back moment." What does it look like?

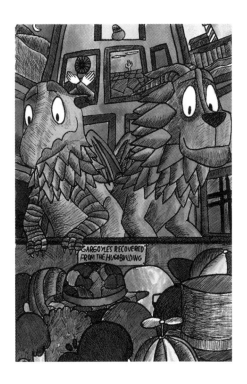

GARGOYLES RECOVERED
FROM THE HUGO BUILDING

CHAPTER SIXTEEN

"Sir, you must eat something."

Walter barely heard Morton speak and waved his hand at him as if to send him away.

"As you wish, sir," Morton intoned as he left with a bowl and a spoon. Walter's head was turned towards the window. The snowfall was turning into a winter storm.

"Snow reminds me of Hunky. I wonder how Hunky is doing? Is he cold?" No sooner did Walter finish his thought than the window crashed open. Walter sat straight up in his bed. He was startled but not frightened. He stared in disbelief when a pigeon flew into the room. Walter thought to himself, "How could a pigeon survive a snow storm like this?"

Hunky, followed by Boss, jumped into the room from the open window. When they both hit the wooden floor, it created a loud boom.

Morton screamed from the hallway, "Are you all right, sir?"

Walter smiled. "Yes, Morton, go back to bed. I dropped my...uh...bowling ball."

"Your what sir?" Morton yelled.

"Morton, go back to bed. Everything is all right. Tomorrow I will take my breakfast in the dining room."

"Yes sir!" Morton replied excitedly as his footsteps faded down the hall.

"Well, you are a sight for these old eyes, Hunky!" Walter exclaimed.

"Walter, this is Boss and Don, my very dear friends."

Walter looked at Boss. He saw her broken ear and her moss-covered legs. He thought she was beautiful and perfect. Don's family started to fly into the room one by one. In moments, there were dozens of pigeons all over the room.

"OK everyone, let's gooooo!" Don ordered, waving his wings and directing the pigeons back to the window. "I assume, sizing up the size of this joint, you have some sort of coop or aviary where we can crash?" Don queried, looking directly at Walter.

"Oh, yes, of course, around the back." Walter shook his head. "I guess a talking pigeon isn't so strange after a talking gargoyle," he declared to no one in particular. As quickly as they flew in, the pigeons were gone.

Walter looked at Hunky with wide eyes. "Hunky, are you staying? I mean, are you both staying? I have plenty of room for both of you."

Boss smiled at Walter and back at Hunky. "Yes, we are staying."

Walter built Boss a beautiful stand just like Hunky's. Don and his family remained on the property, too. Walter's new family filled him with love and a sense of purpose. He no longer felt the need for a large home. So, he moved into a cozy apartment on his property adjacent to the main building and donated his mansion to the City of Metanoia.

The city's leaders turned Walter's former home into a museum and hired Morton, Walter's faithful servant, to be the curator. Unaware of what went on in his museum after nightfall, Morton found it strange to find feathers all about the ballroom each morning but he never really investigated. He simply had them cleaned up each day in preparation for a new crop of visitors. Guests of all ages toured the museum and would continue to do so for years.

By day, visitors admired the gargoyles. By night, the museum was a home to a most unique group of friends.

Discussion Questions

Do you have a Walter Christensen (W.C.) in your life?

What does he represent in the book?

Walter certainly could have put Hunky and Boss on his roof like they were used to for centuries. Why do you think he chose to have them remain inside instead?

EPILOGUE

You are never stuck if you believe in yourself.

Even if you stop believing in yourself for a while, your friends will help you through.

Sometimes you are somewhere too long and just have to go.

Friendship is the family you choose.

And family is the only thing that lasts.

The End

ABOUT THE AUTHOR

"Work-life balance is a myth.
Work-life management is a solution!"

Andrea Mower's thesis is based on three decades of professional experience in human capital across a variety of industries. An accomplished executive, consultant, published author, and speaker, Andrea brought her HR journey to life in *Boss & Hunky: The Adventures of an Out-of-Work Gargoyle*, which was inspired by the many characters she encountered in business and in the arts. Andrea has a proclivity for examining human behavior, an innate quality that fuels both her creativity and business acumen.

An actress since childhood, she earned a bachelor's degree in Theater from the University of the Arts, studying under Camille Paglia, directed by Walter Dallas. For all of her adult life, Andrea has performed alongside her husband Tim as half of Timand Productions, presenting magic shows and historical reenactments for audiences large and small around the world. Her favorite performance was before an audience of 10,000. Her litany of successful roles includes print work, promotional spokes modeling, corporate videos, and her bucket-list achievement of performing in the off-Broadway premier of the musical "O Night Divine" in 2010. In 2004, she partnered with concert pianist Dr. Ori Steinberg to release the holiday album "Snow."

With a keen sense of behavioral dynamics and practice in all aspects of human resources, Andrea ascended to the roles of Chief Human Resources Officer and Chief Administrative Officer. The second act of her career has involved putting her proven leadership skills to work assisting organizations with their most valuable asset, PEOPLE.

In 2017, she launched HR Goddess, a human resources consulting practice. From professional development, employee recruitment, and employee retention to organizational structure, compensation and performance management systems, and strategic planning, Andrea is a sought-after consultant and partner to organizations in a variety of industries, including medical media, government, and manufacturing. Lighthearted and engaging, Andrea incorporates theatrics into corporate meetings, seminars, and talks. Partnering with Andrea guarantees a professional and fresh approach tailored to the client, audience, and topic.

Andrea earned her master's degree in Organization Leadership from Cabrini University. She is PHR and SHRM-CP certified and was a Delaware Valley nominee for HR Person of the Year. As a longtime member of the Chester County Human Resources Association, Andrea served three years on the Board of Directors as Vice President, President, and past President.

In addition to writing, singing, and acting, Andrea enjoys drawing, painting, and spending time at the beach with Tim and their Bouvier des Flanders Thurston Howl. While she enjoyed entertaining children as Sweetheart the Clown early in her career, it might take some prodding to get her back in the oversized clown suit and shoes.